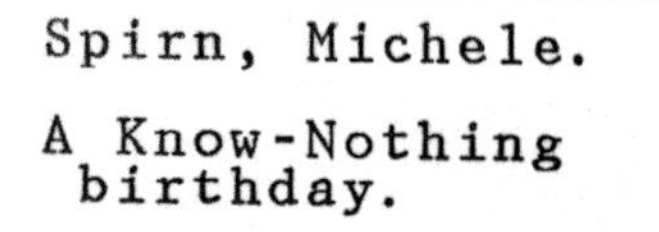

Spirn, Michele.

A Know-Nothing birthday.

An I Can Read Book®

A KNOW-NOTHING BIRTHDAY

story by Michele Sobel Spirn
pictures by R. W. Alley

HarperCollinsPublishers

For Mom and Dad—Norma and Marvin Spirn—
and for Steve and Josh, as always
—M.S.S.

For Jared, whose birthday came
while the paint was still wet.
—R.W.A.

A Know-Nothing Birthday

Library of Congress Cataloging-in-Publication Data
Spirn, Michele.
A Know-Nothing birthday / story by Michele Sobel Spirn ;
pictures by R. W. Alley
p. cm. — (An I can read book)
Summary: Four foolish friends called the Know-Nothings have a birthday celebration.
ISBN 0-06-027273-2. — ISBN 0-06-027274-0 (lib. bdg.)
[1. Birthdays—Fiction. 2. Friendship—Fiction. 3. Humorous stories.]
I. Alley, R. W. (Robert W.), ill. II. Title. III. Series.
PZ7.S7567K1 1997 96-18372
[E]—dc20 CIP
AC

---

1 2 3 4 5 6 7 8 9 10
❖
First Edition

CONTENTS

BORIS
MORRIS
DORIS
NORRIS

WHOSE BIRTHDAY?

Boris, Morris, Doris, and Norris
were four good friends.
People called them Know-Nothings.
They didn't know much,
but they knew they liked each other.

Boris's birthday was coming.

He was afraid

his friends had forgotten.

He hummed “Happy Birthday.”
“The bees hum so nicely,”
said Doris.

He sent himself birthday cards.

Norris said,

"Gosh, you have a lot of pen pals."

Boris put signs

all over the house.

“Thank you very much,” Morris said,

“but it’s not my birthday.”

Boris tried again.
“I will bake a cake,”
he said to Norris.

Norris told Morris,

but Morris heard,

"Boris fell over a rake."

Morris ran to tell Doris.

"Boris fell over a rake!" he yelled.

Doris heard,

"Boris has an earache."

"We must help Boris," she said.

She got some pills.

Morris took some bandages.

Morris and Doris found

Boris and Norris eating cake.

"Boris, can you hear me?"

asked Doris.

"Of course," said Boris.

"Where's that nasty rake?"

asked Morris.

"What rake?" asked Boris.

"He seems to be all right.

He is eating cake,"

said Doris.

"That's what I told Morris,"

said Norris.

"No, you told me
that Boris had fallen over a rake,"
said Morris.
"And you told me
Boris had an earache," said Doris.

"Boris, are you all right?"
asked Norris.
"I am fine," said Boris.
"We are so happy
you are all right," said Doris.
And the Know-Nothings
gave Boris a big hug.

MANY HANDS

Doris looked at her calendar.

"Tomorrow is Boris's birthday!"

she cried.

"We must give him presents."

"What shall we get him?"

asked Morris.

"We will have to watch Boris
to find out what he wants,"
said Doris.
Morris watched Boris.

Boris was cleaning the windows.
"I could really use
another pair of hands
to help me,"
he said.

"Hands! He wants hands!"
cried Morris.
"What do you mean?"
asked Doris.
"The last time
I saw Boris
he had two hands."
"When I saw him
he had two hands,"
said Norris.
"He had two hands
when I saw him,"
said Morris.

Doris counted.

"That makes six hands.

That gives me an idea,"

she said.

Morris, Norris, and Doris

went to the biggest store in town.

They went in and out and in and out
and in and out and in and out
the revolving door.

"It is very hard

to get into this store," said Morris.

"May I help you?"

asked the saleswoman.

"We want to buy some gloves

for Boris," said Doris.

"Here are some nice ones,"

said the woman.

"We will take six," said Morris.

"One for each of his hands,"

said Doris.

"Boris sounds special,"

said the woman.

"Yes, he's very handy,"

said Morris, Norris, and Doris.

The Know-Nothings tried to leave.
This time they went out and in
and out and in and out and in
the revolving door.
Finally a big crowd pushed them out.

“That was a long ride,”

said Norris.

And Morris, Norris, and Doris
wobbled as they walked home
with their presents for Boris.

SURPRISE!

Doris heard someone

at the front door.

"Surprise!" she yelled.

"What surprise?" asked Norris.

"I am giving Boris
a surprise birthday party,"
said Doris.

"I am surprised," said Norris.

"But you are not Boris," said Doris.

"I love surprise parties,"
said Norris. "Can I help?"

"Sure," said Doris.

They heard someone at the door.

"Surprise!" yelled Doris and Norris.

"What surprise?" asked Morris.

"No surprise," said Doris.

"Why are you yelling *surprise*?"

asked Morris.

"We are giving Boris

a surprise birthday party,"

said Doris.

"Great!" said Morris.

"Can I surprise him too?"

"Okay," said Doris.

"But we have to find Boris

to surprise him."

They looked in the bathtub.

They looked under the beds.

They looked
up the chimney.
No Boris! 
“Where can he be?” asked Morris.
“I don’t know,” said Doris.
“I have an idea,” said Norris.
“Everyone knows
about food for thought.
We will have a snack
to help us think.”
“You are so clever, Norris,”
said Morris.

"Hi," said Boris.

"Boris, what are you doing here?"
asked Morris.

"I am having a birthday party,"
said Boris.

"But we are giving you
a surprise birthday party,"
said Doris.

HAPPY

"I wish you had told me,"

said Boris.

"Now I am busy with my own party."

“What can we do?” asked Norris.

“We could have the surprise party

without Boris,” said Morris.

“That would be a surprise!”

"I know," said Doris.

"Boris can have two parties.

Finish your party, Boris,

then we will surprise you."

"You are so clever, Doris,"

said Boris.

He lit the candles on his cake
and sang "Happy Birthday."
Then he blew them out.
"I am ready now," he said.

"Happy Birthday!"

yelled Morris, Doris, and Norris.

"What a surprise!" cried Boris.

“Open your presents,” said Morris.

Boris opened the first box.

“Gloves! How nice!” he cried.

He opened the second box.

“Gloves again! Twice as nice!”

He opened the third box.

“Gloves! What a clever idea!”

"Thank you," Boris said.

"I thought you had forgotten

my birthday."

"How could we forget?" asked Doris.

"Aren't we your best friends?"

Then Doris, Morris, and Norris

helped Boris blow out

his birthday candles again.

They ate lots of cake.

HAPPY BIRTHDAY

And every now and then
his best friends yelled, "Surprise!"
so that Boris wouldn't forget
it was his birthday.